Dark Night

A.D. HEWITT

This edition first published in paperback by
Michael Terence Publishing in 2022
www.mtp.agency

Copyright © 2022 A.D. Hewitt

A.D. Hewitt has asserted the right to be identified as
the author of this work in accordance with the
Copyright, Designs and Patents Act 1988

ISBN 9781800943506

No part of this publication may be reproduced, stored
in a retrieval system, or transmitted, in any form or
by any means, electronic, mechanical, photocopying,
recording or otherwise, without the prior
permission of the publisher

Cover image
Copyright © Vapi
www.123rf.com

Cover design
Copyright © 2022 Michael Terence Publishing

Contents

Synopsis i

Chapter 1: The Repentance of a Sinner 1

Chapter 2: Alan Develops a New Writing Skill 4

Chapter 3: Alan Tells His Cousin a Story 6

Chapter 4: The Nightmare 9

Chapter 5: Farewell 12

Chapter 6: Midnight Dreams 16

Chapter 7: City Break 19

Chapter 8: Alan Stays at his Uncle's House 24

Chapter 9: The Visitors 26

Chapter 10: The Reading Group 28

Chapter 11: The Party 30

Chapter 12: Times Alone Together 33

Chapter 13: Alan's Obsession 35

Chapter 14: Diners at the Restaurant 37

Chapter 15: The Prayer Group 39

Chapter 16: Alan Stays Another Day at his Uncle's 41

Chapter 17: The Day at the Races 44

Chapter 18: Alan Wrote a Story 46

Chapter 19: Grandchildren's Tea Party 48

Chapter 20: Alan and Rick Pop in at a House 50

Chapter 21 52

Chapter 22 54

Synopsis

Alan was an unhappy boy. He was deserted and rejected at school. He also failed his examinations. His prospects were bleak. He was an unemployed teenager in modern Britain.

Alan liked to read detective stories. He also liked to write stories.

At Sunday School, he used to tell stories to the children. He got a mixed reaction from them. Some of them were interested in listening to his stories. At that age, he was a good storyteller. Storytelling was a passion of his. He developed a gift and talent for storytelling and writing stories. He became fruitful. Some of them hated his stories while others took an interest in listening to his stories, especially his storytelling.

A girl he desired and fancied had snubbed and shunned him. Andrea avoided the reading group. Andrea's friends suggested she should listen to Alan telling them stories. But Andrea rejected and avoided Alan. Feeling apathetic, Andrea had no confidence in his storytelling.

Alan continued to amuse the excitable children with his whimsical and heart-warming tales.

One night at a prayer group, at a prayer meeting, Alan accompanied Andrea home late at night. He walked home with her in the dark.

That night Alan told Andrea a story while accompanying her to her house. He amused her. Her initial reaction was that he's extraordinary, charismatic and special. Andrea grew fond of Alan. She admired and adored him!

Andrea liked him. She desired Alan more than anyone else. Andrea had a desire for love for him!

Andrea attended the reading group. Her attendance was punctual. At the library, she listened with interest to Alan telling them his story.

The other girls desired him with great love! They all have adoration and admiration for him.

Chapter 1:
The Repentance of a Sinner

One day, Alan, a young man, asked a woman out. The young woman rejected him. Going back home, he stayed alone in his bedroom. He sulked and was tearful. Alan was deeply sad and very unhappy.

On another day, an evangelist came to visit Alan at his house. Initially, an acquaintance arranged it out of sympathy. (The evangelist became a missionary years later.)

"Why don't you go to church?" he said.

"I don't believe. If I could only believe. What is the point? With my beliefs, I am sceptical. I do have my doubts, of course," replied Alan.

"Why don't you plead? Ask Jesus to come into your life!"

Alan felt apathetic about repentance.

"What good is that going to do? I just don't believe."

"You must plead. You must repent. Why don't you go to church this Sunday? I will be there. You must try."

Alan shrugged. "I don't know," he frowned.

The evangelist took out a Holy Bible. He looked at the New Testament. He read verses from the scriptures.

"You must read your bible. Do get into the habit of reading your bible every day. You must find the time to read it."

Alan felt much better after the evangelist's visit. He would try and make the effort to go to church this Sunday.

Before the evangelist left, he prayed. Alan thanked him and watched him leave.

The evangelist made a commitment to visit him. Alan did not appreciate this. He took it for granted.

* * *

That Sunday church service, Alan attended church. He was met by the evangelist who welcomed him on arrival.

Alan sat down with churchgoers and the congregation. During the Sunday Service, the pastor delivered a sermon from the pulpit. He condemned the congregation for their sinful ways. The pastor referred to it as Armageddon and Apocalypse.

"All this Hell damnation. Well, is this where you want to go? To live in Hell. Your souls burn in Hell. Repent of your sins. Seek salvation and redemption. Follow Christ. Repent of your sins. Take up your cross and follow me. You're living your last days, so, follow the King. Do not be afraid. Come and worship me. You will be fearless. You children. Follow me. I will lead you to the path of righteousness. Do not be afraid. Be God-fearing. Don't live Christless lives. Don't live in darkness. See the light. Don't fall short of the glory of

God. Follow Christ. Through me you have life. Peace, joy, pasture and happiness. Don't die in sin. Don't be condemned to Hell. Your souls in damnation. Believe in me. Repent of your sins. Christ will forgive you. You will be born again. My children. Don't look back. Go marching onwards into battle. In my name profess and proclaim thy name of Christ. Love thy neighbour. Love your brother and sister. Live in peace. With all! The Brotherhood and Sisterhood. Love thy God. Love thy neighbour."

After the church service had ended, the evangelist came up to the middle aisle where Alan was seated.

Alan was disturbed by the sermon. It's a controversial sermon. A frightening one!

"Don't be alarmed. Believe," said Christian.

"It's powerful stuff," replied Alan.

Alan observed the congregation who were disturbed, shaken and alarmed. He took observational notice of them. He took observance of the most noticeable ones in reverence. Most of the congregation was silent, speechless and quiet.

Alan, in a disturbed state, was among the first to leave the church. He did intend to come back to church again. The zealot showed such enthusiasm and keenness to come again to church. He was keen to join a nurture group and prayer group. He regarded the evangelist as a moralist!

Chapter 2:
Alan Develops a New Writing Skill

Alan reflected on his life. He looked back on his sinful life. He used to watch bad films on television and also at the cinema when he and his friend used to go to London to watch the latest motion pictures on release. These films made him corrupt and depraved.

He reflected on the burglary at his house. How his ransacked house caused him to steal and shoplift.

One day, he was caught and arrested by the police for shoplifting. Since that day, he never stole nor shoplifted ever again. He reformed.

Another thing he experienced was that Public Examinations are a hoax!

He failed all of his examinations. He did not get his qualifications to enable him to get educational requirements for certain vacancies. He obtained ungraded in all of his subjects.

Alan left school as a school leaver, enrolling at college. He became unemployed. His future looked bleak with no prospects. He faced unemployment.

In his spare time, he wrote stories. He had a passion for writing stories, although they were mediocre. He developed a skill for writing, It became an enjoyable interest of his.

Dark Night

After writing to occupy himself with his occupational interest, Alan rounded off the day by watching television. He watched a good film.

The next day, his cousin and his friends come round. Alan welcomed his cousin with a deep appreciative love and he acknowledged his cousin's friends with a Boy Scout honour. The gesturer makes a gesture of one. (One of his cousin's friends used to belong to the Boy Scouts.)

Going out in the garden together, they sat down on garden chairs somewhere in the garden, full of shrubbery and plants. A shady spot towards the middle of the garden.

"Why don't you tell us a story?" urged Timmy.

"Yeah. Why don't you?" insisted Paul.

Alan was pressurised to tell a story which he had agreed to tell them. Sitting at an angle, surrounded by all of them, he began to tell them a story, despite it being corny and mediocre, as well as enchanting and whimsical.

With attentiveness, they all sat and listened with interest. They all seemed to like the story which Alan told them.

Alan amused and entertained them. They liked being with their friend. Alan enjoyed his time with them and being together with his cousin again after his separation from his father.

Chapter 3:
Alan Tells His Cousin a Story

On a winter's day, Alan spent time with Gavin, his cousin. They both stayed indoors in the cosy house, sitting in front of the fire, keeping themselves warm. They both warmed up from the fire. The weather outside was cold.

Gavin hoped Alan would tell him another story. Gavin enjoyed listening to Alan telling him stories.

"Tell me a story. Anything," insisted Gavin.

Gavin was charmed by Alan's storytelling. Gavin liked to listen to him telling stories.

"Once upon a time, the dwarves were cursed. Kale, a boy, one day did gardening with the dwarves. He worked with a red-nosed dwarf with big feet. Kale befriended the little dwarf. They both developed a good friendship! The dwarf never received love before. Especially human love! Was this spell broken?

On another day, Kale was threatened by other boys. He was afraid they would attack him. His friend, the little dwarf, protected him. He defended him.

One day, after Kale had done gardening, he got hopelessly lost in the woods. Then the dwarf appeared by magic in the woods. The dwarf showed him out of the woods. Kale had been lost and then found in the haunted woods.

Whilst on his travels, the boy had nowhere to stay and live. The dwarf by magic built a log cabin. There the happy boy lived in the cabin. He called it his home.

The forest and meadows were enchanting, with a nearby stream. Kale loved it here. Kale and the dwarf had such love for each other. They formed a good friendship. The dwarf, with big feet, was very happy. He'd found a friend. The spell was broken. The dwarf was free at last! The red-nose dwarf's spirit was set free. The dwarf formed a strong love. A bond with the boy. His deep spiritual love was so precious and so great it broke all curses!

The dwarves moved land. They lived all together on the land. The emerald forest. A magical enchantment!

All of the dwarves and Kale lived happily ever after.

Gavin enjoyed the whimsical story.

"Wait until I tell Paul and Timmy. They would love to hear it!" said the cousin excitedly.

"Would they? It makes a change from my dumb stories!"

"How do you get inspired? What gives you your inspiration?"

Alan remembered his childhood fascinations.

"Watching animation. I used to sneak downstairs in the middle of the night. My father used to wait for me to come to put on a projector. I used to watch old black and white cartoons and animation. I just loved it."

"Yes. I remember. I have seen the cartoons and animation myself. It's wonderful! Isn't it nostalgic!" exclaimed his cousin, elated.

Alan remembered it with a sentimental joy.

"It's a joy! A treat and delight. I will never forget it. It's a childhood inspiration."

Chapter 4:
The Nightmare

Alan got up late. He woke up at midday. He had a lie-in. Last night, Alan had a bad nightmare.

He got up and got dressed and went into the lounge. His mother was seated in the armchair, looking at a woman's magazine. The fashion photography of the naturally photogenic models posing with elegance. Their poise was natural.

"Son, did you sleep well?"

"No. I didn't. I had a nightmare," he replied.

"Son, what's wrong?"

Alan's voice sounded hoarse. "My father left me. Don't go! Don't leave me, I said."

"Your father doesn't love me. Nor does he love you. He's in love with another woman," said Mother, ashamed.

"Damn! My father has gone. I don't have a father."

Mrs Watkins put her arms around her son. "You have got your mum."

Alan held his mother tightly. Mrs Watkins passionately squeezed her son, a tight squeeze around his waist.

"I won't get over my dad. You won't get over your husband."

"I don't think either of us ever will. Will we? Your father has his woman. He has got his own life now. He doesn't care about you. His interest is his woman. Isn't it?"

Alan was infuriated. "I don't want to dwell on it. I don't want to even think about it."

"Your father has abandoned you. He has walked out of our lives," said Mother miserably.

Alan felt angered by his father's desertion.

"I hate my father. I don't think I will love him after this."

"Who will? I will kill him," snapped Mother.

"My father never cared about me. Did he? He never loved me," sulked Alan.

"Your father disowned you. He deserted you."

"He only cared about the Hound and Duck. And having affairs," he moaned.

"Your father wanted a daughter. He never got it. Your father was loyal in business. But unfaithful."

"Just typical!" he tutted. "I hate him. He's no father of mine. Is he?"

"Your father liked the nightlife. He likes nightclubbing. That's how we met."

Alan had a sarcastic tone in his voice, "Was it. Was it

really?"

"Your father was immoral."

"You could say that again. I will never love again. Who will love me?" he said sadly.

"*I* love you. Your mum loves you."

"Do you really?"

Mrs Watkins cuddled her son. Her affectionate tenderness was motherly. "Son, I do love you, boy."

The son took comfort from his mother's love. Realising how deep the love his passionate mother had for him. Alan cherished his moments alone with his mother. His time with his mother was quite bittersweet as he reflected on his past and everything else at present.

Going back to his bedroom, he stayed there. Alan remained housebound. As a loner. He was disturbed at being all by himself.

He reflected on his father. Not really having any love for his father. The son unloved his father. He was at present abandoned and deserted by his father. He felt alienated from his father. He hated his father. He bore a grudge against his father. He pondered on his father. In deep reflection, he thought back to his parents' separation and divorce. Since that time, his father had deserted him!

Chapter 5:
Farewell

Leaving the main school building at lunchtime, Alan headed down to the playground. There, somewhere in the playground, he waited for Malcolm to come. Expecting Malcolm, a schoolfellow, to come anytime now.

At this time, the playground was less and less full of schoolchildren. It was less crowded at this time.

Malcolm still came with the amicable intention of saying farewell to Alan before leaving school for the last time!

Alan stood still while waiting for Malcolm. He passed time away by daydreaming. The pupils in the playground today were from the First Years to the Fourth Years. The pupils stayed in groups amongst themselves. Every school year occupied different parts of the playground. (Some of the Fifth Years had already left school. They were school leavers!)

Alan looked at the younger pupils. The female pupils were naïve, playful, childlike and innocent. They were talkative while staying in groups all around some areas of the playground.

Alan waited, expecting Malcolm to come. He came on time to see Alan. Alan saw Malcolm walking towards him.

Dark Night

"It's time. I will be leaving," said Malcolm.

"So soon!" uttered Alan.

"Farewell!" said Malcolm.

Alan walked up closer to Malcolm. He rested his hand on Malcolm's shoulder. Malcolm reminded Alan that he would be leaving school. That today was his very last day at school. Any minute now, Malcolm intended to depart from school. His departure was punctual and on time.

"I shouldn't say this, but today is my last day here," reminded Malcolm.

"It's mine as well," mumbled Alan.

Alan was fully aware of pupils looking at them. Malcolm, a school leaver. He was deeply sad at watching Malcolm walk away. Leaving school for the very last time. Alan was very sad at watching Malcolm go.

In a few days, Alan followed suit by leaving school after he had sat his examinations. Alan was glad it was over. He had such a miserable and unhappy time at his comprehensive school. Alan was destined to fail all of his examinations. It's all doom and gloom for him.

Alan remembered his very last day at comprehensive school. Regrettably, it was deeply saddening. That school year he was displeased at his travelling because he didn't have a valid bus pass. He had to keep paying his bus fare every time he boarded the bus.

During those school years, Alan had been suffering from bereavement.

***

A long time ago, Alan left his mother at the Housing Association. Leaving the place. He waited at a bus stop.

As the bus came, he got on board the bus. He paid his bus fare. Going upstairs on the bus. There he met two of the loveliest tanned schoolgirls. Alan swooned at the sight of them. The pubescent teenagers were ravishing beauties.

Before Alan's nervous breakdown and relapse, that remained one of the happiest days of his life!

In retrospect, it was a special moment for him, because at his school he used to be snubbed, shunned and loathed. Furthermore, he failed all of his examinations that summer term.

***

During the summer, Alan stayed at home. His time at school had finally ended.

Mrs Watkins realised he was spending considerably more time at home. She worried about her son.

"How do you feel about school being all over?"

"I am relieved it's over. I am glad it's all over," sighed Alan.

Mrs Watkins thought of the memories of school. Having the philosophical reflection of it. An introspection of it!

"Don't they say that school is the best days of one's lives?" said Mother introspectively.

"That's a matter of opinion. Not for me. Maybe."

"Looking back, you may feel that way."

"I don't feel that way at all. I am glad it's over."

His mother discarded her son's school uniform. Some of the new school clothes he had been bought he just did not wear. All those new clothes were a waste of money. A superstition!

All alone by himself at home, Alan reflected on his schooldays. Looking back at his schooldays, they were a misery and an unhappiness. His memories of school were unhappy, miserable and bittersweet.

Chapter 6:
Midnight Dreams

Since school broke up, Alan had stayed home. He spent more time at home. It was the start of the summer holiday. (He did look forward to going to Spain on his holiday.)

At the weekend, Alan, with nothing else to do, spent time reading a book about monks. He read about the Cistercian, Buddhist and Tibetan monks in the Himalayas, their ancestral Tibetan chants and how they mysteriously walked through walls! The monks lived in a monastery or retreat.

Nowadays, Alan enjoyed the peace and quiet. The solitude, being alone at home. The freedom and isolation of being away from families and people. He kept away from his older brother. He did tend to bully him, and his mother at times was abusive, horrible and nasty. His mother was unsympathetic, showing no sympathy and understanding when he was deeply mournful and bereaved!

Alan liked the quiet life and solitude. Every night he sat out in the garden. The nights were dark. He was peaceful, restful and relaxed. Recovering from fatigue.

The dreamer dreamed, the daydreamer lost in a reverie and trance. He fantasised in the garden. The shining moonlight illuminated the garden. He was enchanted by the glow of the moonshine. The glow of the moonlight was an enchantment. The natural glowing beauty of the garden was a great delight. He took wonder of it. The beauty of it was pure joy. He had never seen anything quite so wonderful! The garden in summertime. Wonderfully beautiful and marvellous. A paradisiacal delight.

With the rose garden. The blooming and blossoming of the rosebuds and roses. The floribunda was marvellously beautiful!

At night, Alan stayed outside in the garden. He sat down on a garden chair with a soft cushion against his back.

He enjoyed his time alone. The season of this glorious summer! He was enchanted by the glow of the garden at midnight. On this sultry night, he could stay out here and dream of paradise!

He wasn't able to do so as he became uncomfortable sitting down for hours.

Alan took joy from peace. The quietude was a pure delight. He felt exhilarated. He felt invigorated by the coolness of the air while sitting in a far corner of the garden. He was enthralled by the summer season. It was a great joy as he took such delight in summer and the marvellous beauty of the glowing garden in the moonlight. The glow of the moonshine was enchanting.

He sweated in the sultry air. The weather felt sticky.

Alan romanticised in the pitch-dark garden. He dreamt of falling in love! He took delight in his romantic fantasies.

The enchantment of the glow of the garden electrified him intensely. His senses became perceptive. He sniffed at the redolent roses in a rose garden.

Going back indoors, Alan went to bed very late at a quarter past one a.m.

Chapter 7:
City Break

Alan left his hotel room. He went to the poolside where his mother was lying on a sun lounger. At that time there were families there and other Europeans. Some women were in the swimming pool and a few others sunbathing, lounging about while engaging in narcissistic eroticism of themselves, relaxing, sunbathing and tanning themselves. Applying suntan lotion on their bodies. Others, their tanned skin glossy and their bodies glistening from drops of water. Two of them suntanned and another one beautifully bronzed. Her figure was admirably lovely and suntanned. A Mediterranean.

Alan envied them. They seemed to be happy, blissful, laid-back and carefree. They took no notice of him. They were not interested in the foreigner. They did not desire the undesirable man. Alan had acne. Alan took an interest in one of them. This young woman was alluring and enticing. She attracted attention. She dived into the swimming pool gracefully. The woman swam with a few other women. Her beauty was desirable and admirable. The nymph's voluptuousness a desirably appealing irresistibleness. Her bronze suntanned figure appeared from the rippling water. The Austrian-? The Spaniard's curvaceous body exposed when revealed in the water. Her body glistening with drops of water.

Alan desired the sexy European! He preferred her to

anyone else. Was she single, and unmarried?

Alan tried to fully understand female sexuality. Their prurience and erotomania. The narcissistic obsessions and parading exhibitionism of females. The pleasure-seekers attracting attention. The wanton married women lounging by the poolside with or without their husbands.

Alan soon lost interest in going to the poolside. He became utterly bored with doing nothing. He felt unloved and unwanted. So, he decided to leave his mother alone and go back to his hotel room.

Feeling hot, Alan cooled down in the shady, cool hotel room. The net curtains covered the windows. He lay down on his bed and rested. In the coolness of the fresh air. His body was sweaty and he felt dehydrated and rather thirsty. He felt faint, dizzy and nauseous. He dozed. Alan felt tired and weary. He was unused to the climate and terrain. He was excited by the strange surroundings and paradisiacal location.

Feeling enervated, Alan stayed the rest of the day in the hotel. He relaxed. Enjoying his time all alone. Later he dined at the restaurant with his mother. The diners were families and romantic couples deeply in love. Honeymooners in love having a romance while staying at the hotel.

Alan rounded off the night by watching television in his hotel room with room service. He enjoyed himself.

During the course of the week, Alan saw the attractive woman, a continental! With a beautiful figure.

He saw her only a few times. The last time when the woman dined out at the hotel restaurant with her handsome husband. Despite his shock. He felt terrible disapproval at finding out she was married. His disenchantment was an unpleasantness. He was glad that the married couple checked out during the afternoon. "Good riddance!"

That Friday afternoon he met his mother in the lobby near Reception. His mother sat alone in the seating area while looking at a magazine. The glossy pictures of the naturally photogenic fashion models. Mrs Watkins spent time reading a magazine. An agony column.

"How has your day been? How are you finding it?" wondered Mother.

"It's a lovely day. Isn't Spain a beautiful country? I love it here. It makes a change from England. The Spanish are friendly. The senoritas are lovely. The food and drink and nightlife are good. Listening to the Spanish guitarist was brilliant. I just love the guitar. The Spanish music. I like to sightsee. I just love the beaches. Isn't it glorious! I would love to live here. Wouldn't you? The weather is great in Spain. It's lovely. There are fine restaurants and really good nightclubs. I haven't been to Ibiza. I really want to go and check out the nightclubbing scene. Yeah. Really. I like paella. I love the oranges and lemon grove trees. I love the orange juice. I love Seville. I like the castle. I like the places of interest and historic attractions," said son excitedly.

"Son, I am glad you are liking your holiday here."

Mrs Watkins put the magazine down on the table with a pile of magazines and a supplement. Losing interest, Mrs Watkins became distracted by a holidaymaker with his luscious wife and playful son and daughter in the lobby.

"Come on! Let's go to the beach," urged Mother.

"Can we?" said son childishly.

Alan felt a childish excitement.

"Yippee!" he said, excitedly.

Leaving the foyer, mother and son came out of the hotel. They both came to the concrete long road. They both walked down the endless road. There they reached the beautiful beach. The beach was crowded with holidaymakers. Everywhere on the sandy beach, there were families, loungers and sunbathers. The countrymen, inhabitants and locals may have been Spaniards and Iberians who came to the beach that glorious day. The energetic children played. They made such big sandcastles. There along the shore, a nun chaperoned a group of girls walking along the beach.

Mrs Watkins and her son walked down the beach. They both stopped at an unoccupied spot. They lounged on the beach but within minutes they had been intruded on. They both got up from the scorching sand and strolled down the beach. They kept strolling until they both had had enough of strolling. Reaching the end of the beach, they both turned and made their way back to the hotel. The hotel promoted classical music, a performance of the latest promotion.

Dark Night

Later they both stayed in a hotel room. They both cooled down in the shade. Outside the blazing sun was scorching. It was sweltering.

Alan got deep inner peace and joy at going on holiday to Mallorca. He reflected on his deep philosophical reflection.

"It's great to be in Spain. We have spent most of our time in England. We are ignorant about life abroad. How about overseas?"

"Nowadays it's pretty expensive to go on holiday. People simply just don't have the money," said Mother matter-of-factly.

"I feel free and at peace here. Actually, I could stay here forever. I wish it would never end," sighed son.

Alan sat out on the balcony in a dreamy state watching the sunset. He admired the incredibly lovely view. The great sight was amazingly breathtaking. He admired the view of the celestial skies overhead. From where he stood at an angle from the balcony. In an opposite position from the terrace. He admired the glorious and sublime sunset.

Going to bed late that Spanish night, Alan slept peacefully and woke up late the next day. He had completely forgotten about his dream last night. He still did not remember his sweet dream of a paradisiacal significance!

After their break here, they rounded off the week by staying somewhere else. A charming, picturesque village deep in the mountains.

Chapter 8:
Alan Stays at his Uncle's House

At his uncle's house, Alan stayed in. He stayed up late at night. That night he could not sleep. He sneaked out of the side door and walked into the large garden late at night. The garden was illuminated. Illumination by the moonlight. The enchantment of the glowing moonshine.

Alan was enchanted by the glow of the moonlight. The garden looked lovelier from the enchantment of the summer night. Alan enjoyed the summertime at his uncle's home. This summer long.

Alan walked around the garden in circles, then walked up and down the garden. He cherished his time at his uncle's. He liked the quietude. He took joy from the languor. At this time the garden was quieter, darker and pitch-dark with the house lights on. The lights reflected in the dark shadows. He breathed in the fresh air. The air felt cool and sticky. He admired the beauty of the garden in summertime. He felt exhilarated.

Alan was all alone at home. He liked to be alone. He felt excited at being free at present. With a sense of freedom. With no restrictions imposed on him by his mother. His uncle made allowances for Alan.

Alan stayed every night out in the garden. The nights were dark. He sat out in the garden. He gazed at the starry skies. He star-gazed at the skies. He took wonder at star-gazing. He had an interest in Astronomy. Amongst the constellations did he catch sight of a shooting star?

Sitting on a garden chair for a long time. He felt uncomfortable sitting for long periods.

He got up and stretched his legs. He wandered around the garden with purposeless aimlessness.

He took a look at a moon dial and a fountain as well as the vegetable patch by the greenhouse.

In the dark, Alan walked back to the house. The lights reflected in the darkness and shadows.

Alan was unafraid of being alone in a big house. He was so used to staying in a big house by himself.

That moonlit night Alan went to bed. The summer night long. The invitingness a pleasure.

Chapter 9:
The Visitors

One afternoon Alan walked out into the garden. He admired the really beautiful garden. He looked at the borders and flowerbeds. They ranged from flowers, herbaceous borders, shrubs and plants. From the rose bushes everywhere in the garden.

All of the roses were so beautiful, including the rosebuds. All of the colours of the loveliest roses brilliant in the shining sun. The radiance a resplendence.

The gardener kept the garden impeccably immaculate.

Suddenly, Alan heard laughter and hysteria. The few women were in hysterics.

That sunny afternoon Alan's aunt had visitors. Alan entered the Victorian house. There he met his aunt waiting for him. His aunt welcomed Alan. Going into the living room, he met strangers. His aunt introduced him to them.

"This is my nephew, Alan."

Monique and Jeanette shook Alan's hand.

"Pleased to meet you," they said.

Alan's aunt, Monique and Jeanette sat down. They had tea together. Alan joined them for tea. He enjoyed having tea with them. Sitting down and listening to their conversation. Alan remained silent, shy and diffident. His aunt, Monique and Jeanette, mother and daughter conversed together.

Jeanette looked at Alan and paid attention to him.

"What did you do today?"

"I played soldiers," replied Alan.

"Who with?" asked Jeanette, perplexed.

"By myself. I am a King."

"Well, that makes me a Queen. Aren't you a Prince?"

"No. I am King of the Castle," retorted Alan.

Jeanette was engaged at present.

"Alan, it's nice to have met you. Really it is. I must talk to your aunt now. That's why we've come."

His aunt was losing patience.

"Now Alan, leave us. Let us talk," urged Aunt.

Alan had overstayed his welcome. He got up and left them alone. He went upstairs in a daydreamy state. Sliding his hand on the bannister. He stayed in his bedroom. He reflected on Monique and Jeanette. He rather liked them. He hoped he would see them both again. On reflection spending time with them again would be pleasing.

Chapter 10:
The Reading Group

Alan attended a reading group at the library. He was disappointed at Andrea not attending the reading group this time. The reading group chose a selection of books for recommendation. The most popular one was a historical novel. The reading group consisted mostly of females. They had a passion for reading. They had an interest in romance. At present, it's the most popular category amongst female readers.

Alan preferred a crime novel or a detective novel. He was not interested in a romance or a historical novel. Alan had much more interest in crime novels than anything else.

Alan enjoyed reading. He had a passion for writing and storytelling. This reading group consisted of professionals. They may have once been academics, scholars as well as intellectuals. Every reader had an interest in the classics and English literature. This reading group talked about a particular book they were currently reading. Every reader recommended a historical novel. The second choice was a romance.

Alan felt agitated and displeased. He had lost interest in reading now. He was distracted by movement around him. He was too upset about Andrea being absent from this reading group. He seemed relatively disappointed at

Andrea's absence.

He expected Andrea to attend the reading group. Alan did wonder if Andrea had dropped out? He used to like her. Now he resented her. Alan had a disregard for her absence.

Andrea shunned him!

Perhaps she does have a good reason for her absence from the reading group today.

Chapter 11:
The Party

Mrs Watkins and her son had been invited to a party. Mrs Watkin's friend, Gill, said she was welcome to invite her son.

At the party later that evening, there were many strangers. Alan did not know these strangers. He felt uneasy and uncomfortable not knowing them.

Alan had met the host of the party a few times now. He hadn't met her daughter before. Today was the very first time. Maybe the last ever time!

The party food was served. Alan did not eat any of it as he's a vegetarian. The music blared out. There was dancing. Everybody else danced. Alan did not dance. He had inhibitions. They danced better than he did. Alan was too embarrassed to dance.

Earlier, he and his mother had commuted to get to Gill's house. His mother made friends with Gill at church. He felt too enervated to dance.

One lovely woman gained and received all of the attention. Alan envied the adored woman.

Out in the small garden, Alan met all of the children. At that time the children preferred their own company rather than the company of adults.

The quiet children did not talk at this present time.

At present, they weren't childishly conversational in the presence of everybody out there in the garden. They were bored at having nothing else to do. They felt unenthusiastic and uninterested in everything.

The adults dictated to them. Of course, the children had to obey and behave themselves. All of the obedient children avoided the adults. Staying in groups amongst themselves.

Alan wondered if the children would like to hear him tell a story to them. He asked them. The glum children were friendly and enthusiastic.

They all gathered around Alan. All of the children listened with interest as Alan told them a story.

The children became excited, filled with excitement and joy. They were all thrilled and enthralled listening to his fairy-tale. All of them left the party in a good mood. Their parents picked them up.

Gill told everybody to leave. It was her house. Gill's daughter's birthday?

Alan wasn't pleased the party had ended. He was disappointed by everyone leaving. He and his mother ended up staying the night at Gill's house.

Leaving the house, the next morning, Alan had forgotten his cardigan which he had left on a chair in the spare bedroom. The cardigan smelled of antiperspirant.

They travelled back home.

Later that night, Alan stayed in his bedroom. He mused on the children. It gave him great pleasure and satisfaction telling the children a fairy-tale that he had made up.

He wondered if the children had liked his stories or whether they disliked them immensely. Nonetheless, the storyteller had dreamt them up. The children felt a thrilling excitement from being told stories. They loved stories.

Chapter 12:
Times Alone Together

One day a small group from the church went to the high street to go to the department store restaurant on the third floor.

They all sat down at different tables. Preferring their own company of friends rather than mixing with other people.

Alan sat with his friend, Perry Thorpe. The luxury restaurant was air-conditioned. The restaurant was beautiful. It was fine and luxurious the restaurant. The department store was local. An hour earlier his friend Perry had popped into his house. They would both go to the department store restaurant for tea. They both enjoyed the nice times there. It was a really lovely experience. A pleasant one.

"Isn't it lovely! It's so hot," gasped Perry.

"It's lovely weather. We have to make use of it."

Perry was pretentious. He was unconcerned.

"Do you think you will backslide?"

"I don't know. I hope not."

"How about them?" asked Perry, pointing.

"I won't comment. I won't judge. Condemn and be condemned. I shouldn't judge. Shouldn't one get one's own house in order? One shouldn't make judgements. Nor condemn."

"Backsliding seems to be the thing. People come and go," remarked Perry.

"I agree. They don't stay. Nor do they last. Temptation and desire take over. Don't they? Those worldly desires!"

"Do you worry?"

"Of course, I worry. Who doesn't? I worry about my life. My future. If you're right with Christ. You shouldn't worry!"

Something distracted Perry's attention. A woman's fine figure, beautifully tanned.

"How about that woman?"

"What woman?" asked Alan, puzzled.

"Andrea."

"Do you like her?"

"I have seen her."

"She won't last. She will backslide as the others do."

They both drank their tea. They both cooled down from the air-conditioning. They enjoyed the luxuriousness of the modern restaurant. They both stayed a short time in the restaurant.

Leaving the restaurant together, they both went home. The next day Perry popped in to see Alan again.

Chapter 13:
Alan's Obsession

Alan looked at the chess game. He studied the next chess moves. From the subsequent chess moves, the Blacks attacked the defence. Penetrating the defence, from offensive to counter-attack.

Finally, the Black Queen checkmated the White King, exposed and defenceless on that particular flank.

"You are a clever boy!" praised Mother.

Alan lay the King flat on the chessboard.

"I am a King! And Jeanette my Queen. I am a King when I play soldiers. I too live in a castle."

"Son, you do have an imagination. All these boys' games you play. You really ought to grow up and be a responsible adult," admonished Mother.

"Seriously, I am a King. Jeanette my Queen. We are King and Queen," said Alan chivalrously.

"Shouldn't you be Prince and Princess?" laughed Mother.

"Oh! Whatever!" said son, flustered.

"My son a King. It's quite possible you'll be regal."

"Yes, Mother. I will. Bow!" he clapped.

Mrs Watkins slapped her son's hand.

"Dear, you're talking to your mother. This is reality. The real world."

Feeling exhausted, Alan sat in the armchair. Suddenly his mother left him alone. Alan dozed off in the silence of the room. The carriage clock slowed.

He woke up about an hour and a half later. With his blurry vision, he then saw a chess piece on the sideboard. The King reminded him of his obsession with regality and the Knight and his chivalries.

Chapter 14:
Diners at the Restaurant

Mrs Watkins and her son and Jeanette and her mother had gone out for the night. They dined out at a restaurant. They sat at a reserved table. In a fine restaurant. The waiter handed them a menu each. They each ordered first from a menu.

Mrs Watkins, Jeanette and her mother drank fine wine. Alan drank mineral water.

The waiter came back to take their order from the menu. They each chose from a menu, à la carte.

Jeanette and her mother were gourmets and Alan and Mrs Watkins diners. Alan took delight in his nice treat while Jeanette and her mother took it for granted. They were both so used to the high life and glamour.

Alan liked them. He liked their company. He had never experienced anything like this before!

He enjoyed the novelty. He wondered how long their friendship would last.

Alan remained silent. He enjoyed his time at the restaurant. He was not interested in their conversation. He appeared overwhelmed. He took joy from his treat.

During their long conversation, Alan daydreamed. He engaged in a daydreamy reverie.

Leaving the restaurant, they got into a vintage car. Alan and Mrs Watkins were dropped off at home.

Alan remembered his night out with Jeanette and her mother. He had a good time with them. The glamorous duo.

Chapter 15:
The Prayer Group

Alan attended the church service. He sat in the middle row, facing the front of the pulpit and church.

During the Sunday Service, the born-again Christians gave their personal testimonies.

The congregation and church-goers sang hymns and songs.

The pastor gave a sermon about spiritual warfare. The end days.

When the service ended, Alan got up and took in everybody else. He spotted Andrea and her mother somewhere near the back row, standing at the front of two chairs by a row of chairs on that side of an aisle.

They were both talking to two members of the congregation. These were regular church-goers.

Alan came up to them. Interrupting their conversation. Andrea and her mother both stopped talking. They paid heed to Alan. Alan was surprised that Andrea had come to church today. He had not expected them to attend this church today.

"What are you doing in church today?"

"The glass mirror will crack," replied Andrea.

"How did you find the service?" asked Alan.

"It was heavy."

"It's about Armageddon. One can't compromise."

"So it is," mumbled Andrea. "I am going to a prayer group straight after."

"You are? Me too," smiled Alan.

They gathered around and talked for some time.

Afterwards, certain individuals got lifts to a prayer group, a prayer meeting held at a house. At that semi-detached house near a railway line and alley. A prayer group gathered. Alan and Andrea joined a prayer group at a house. (Also, the nurture group was now being offered for born-again Christians converted!)

They were both silent during the prayer group (meeting).

The prayer group was worshipful. They all prayed and sang songs. They experienced a night of worship and prayers.

After the prayer group had finished praying, they all rounded off the night by having tea in a cosy house. The people from the prayer group were talkative and the elder conversational.

Alan felt like a zealot tonight in the presence of other zealots and worshippers and prayers.

A few others popped in. These individuals turned up late at the gathering.

Chapter 16:
Alan Stays Another Day at his Uncle's

On a cold winter's day, Alan came into a room. He sat down on a rocking chair in front of the fire. He relaxed comfortably. This used to be the place where his grandfather once sat and told the grandchildren stories.

Alan was deeply saddened as he remembered his grandfather. He grieved for his grandfather. Alan took comfort in sitting comfortably. With his back leaning against a soft cushion and his legs stretched out.

He had deep thoughts in his contemplative state of mind. He nodded off as he took comfort from the heat of the fire. The broad daylight got darker. The weather became much colder. (Outside his breath rose in the air.)

Alan woke up in the dark. From the fireplace, the fire flickered in the dark. The aura had a romantic sensation. He had got cramp from sitting in the same position all the time. He changed his seated position and the position of his stretched-out legs. He stirred from moving the position of his body.

In the dark, Alan got up. He moved to the other side of the wall. He fumbled to switch on the light.

Alan went upstairs to a front bedroom where his cousin made a model plane, a Bomber. He'd painted it well. It was beautifully painted. The Bomber had camouflage.

The table was covered in sheets of newspaper with a painted model plane left to dry on them.

Alan envied his cousin. He had a big collection of model planes; Bombers and Fighters. His cousin had a passion for making models. His cousin was knowledgeable about the Military and Air Force as well as having good knowledge of World War II history, with reference to the models.

Alan picked up a dried Fighter. He raised it in the air. Making childish sounds as he moved about.

"Put it back, you dimwit! You'll break it!" said his cousin reprovingly.

Alan obeyed his cousin and put it back on its stand delicately.

Alan left the spare bedroom to go to his bedroom where he spent the weekend at his uncle's house.

Alan stayed in his bedroom. Enjoying being all alone in his bedroom. He had freedom and privacy again.

His cousin had been picked up by his parent. He had gone home. At that time Alan refused to be driven home.

He wanted to stay another day at his uncle's house.

For a time, Alan enjoyed his freedom and privacy again.

Chapter 17:
The Day at the Races

Alan and his mother and Jeanette and her mother went to the races, a Derby. Alan called himself a Prince. He was given high priority. From the stands, they watched a race. Afterwards, they met jockeys and their horse owners and chic and glamorous ladies somewhere near the racecourse. The fashionable women wore hats and gloves.

The enthusiast asked a question. Alan raised his deep voice.

"Do you have horses?"

"We do have horses," replied Jeanette.

"Can you ride?"

"Oh! Yes! We are good riders," answered Jeanette.

"We have been riding for years," said Mrs Chantelle.

"I can't ride. I have never tried."

"You're missing out. It's an experience," said Jeanette.

Alan observed the jet-set and millionaires amongst the crowds of glamorous women. The Derby glamour. Mixing with the groups of chic women. Alan smiled back at them. Their sweet charmed smiles delighted him. Alan was thrilled and overjoyed at the presence of the jet setters. He probably would not see them ever again. The flamboyant and elegant ladies.

Jeanette and her mother and Alan too got most of the attention. They got high priority of course. That day they were all privileged.

They rounded off the day by going to a fine restaurant. They dined together at the Country Inn. The photographs reminded them of their function and day out at the Derby.

Looking at the colourful photographs together at Rimmington, reminded them of the Derby. It was a truly wonderful day!

They had good memories!

Chapter 18:

Alan Wrote a Story

Alan got depressed thinking of Andrea. At how she rejected him! Thinking of something else. Alan sat at a desk. He concentrated on writing. Suddenly his mother burst into his bedroom. Mrs Watkins disturbed her son. Alan lost his concentration on writing.

"Have you written anything good?"

"Mom, not now. I am trying to write," said her irritated son.

"Do your stories have happy endings?"

"They differ at times. I like to write with a happy ending or something sad. It has to be evocative. I do like a tear-jerker every now and again."

"How is Andrea?"

"Please, Mum. Don't ask. I am trying to get on with my work," muttered her son.

"How is it going between you two?"

Alan's temperament changed. He became melancholic in his frame of mind.

"Andrea doesn't fancy me. She doesn't love me."

"Oh! What a shame. Never mind! My poor boy!"

"Mum, don't!"

Mrs Watkins recalled her response to a marriage proposal.

"I was left on the shelf until your father came. He proposed to me. We wed. Those were the days. Now we've separated and divorced."

"How does it feel to be a divorcee?"

"Now it's lonely. The thing is, I have got my freedom. I don't have any responsibilities or commitments. Only you are my worry."

"Can you go? I am trying to work."

"Why don't you get a job and earn your keep?"

Alan felt humiliated by his mother humiliating him.

"I'll be coming home late tonight. So, you will have to get yourself something to eat."

Alan sighed in relief when his mother left the house to go to work.

He cooled down. He wanted to be alone right now.

That day, Alan wrote pages of a story. From his inspiration, he got the initiative to write, and from his free time too. He allocated a few hours in which to write.

The next day, Alan rewrote his story.

Chapter 19:

Grandchildren's Tea Party

Alan attended the grandchildren's party. During those few hours, they played games: Hide and Seek; Charades; Musical Chairs (the winner received a prize) and Soldiers.

Playing Soldiers in the garden, the children used sticks as weapons. They defended Alan who played the King. They protected Alan from a Brat.

Alan ordered the children. They each obeyed his commands. They guarded him. Obeying his every command. Alan playing the King, made demands on the children who played soldiers, defending him from some of the children, playing the enemy.

Both armies had play fights with sticks. King Alan felt protected by his Army, the children playing soldiers. The Army protected the Princesses playing with their dolls!

The King's Army rounded up the captured prisoners, holding them captive somewhere in the garden. The guards guarded the King.

Later, in the last hour, all the children were invited to a tea party in the garden. They all had such fun together.

Alan enjoyed spending time with the grandchildren. He had such a good time with them.

They played Princesses, Princes and Kings. (One scene in a tower. A castle setting.)

They engaged in a dress rehearsal. A rehearsed masquerade ball scene.

Alan took the golden opportunity to play with the grandchildren and the other children too. It had been some time since he last played with all of them.

Alan professed himself to be a King!

The masqueraders and everybody else around him were his subjects. Of course, they were obedient and obsequious to the King on his throne. He was the King of his Kingdom!

Chapter 20:

Alan and Rick Pop in at a House

Alan and his so-called friend, Rick, popped into Rick's friend's house. Alan stayed with Rick. His so-called friend took all the attention from everybody else. Then he left him with them.

Alan came out into the garden. There he met strangers and acquaintances in the garden.

From the garden, he got a feeling of enchantment and an afterglow.

He came up to Josie standing all alone by a rose bush. Admiring the loveliest roses. The pretentious young woman seemed enticing. A provocative tantaliser!

Josie was not surprised by his presence. She thought of Alan as exposed, vulnerable and spurned. Josie was conceited.

"Will you dance with me?" asked Josie.

"Me! No! You want to dance with me. You don't love me. You never did! I shan't dance with you. I won't. I am going," said Alan bitterly.

Alan walked away and came back indoors. He rejoined Nick and Rick somewhere indoors. In the presence of everybody, Alan felt unwanted and unwelcomed here.

They left the house. Coming here had been regrettably bad. A false pretension. Alan was not invited here again!

Chapter 21:

On a sweltering day, Alan and his mother sat in the shade of the garden. They both cooled down in the shade. They drank cordial in their tumblers.

At this time, Alan preferred to be alone. His mother had intruded on him. Alan objected to his mother invading his privacy. He wanted to spend time alone.

"What's this thing about you being King? People will think you're raving mad," said Mother, smoking.

"I am King. I am King over my soldiers."

"If you insist. You are."

Alan picked up his shield made of thick cardboard. He slipped his fingers through a hole in the cardboard. With his other hand, he stooped down to pick up a stick.

"Put it down. Don't get up to mischief," reprove Mother.

Alan raised a stick in the air.

"I am a King. I will be King!"

"If you say you are."

Sitting in the shade, Alan got blocked in from claustrophobia. He got up. He slipped out of the space between the garden chairs. Somewhere in the open space of the garden, he pretended to have a sword fight.

Dark Night

He was a triumphant and victorious knight in battle. He imagined it.

"I will be King! No one can stop me!" said Alan defiantly.

From Alan imagining himself in a battle (scene).

He fought in battle.

Chapter 22:

Going somewhere in the garden, Jeanette stretched out her hand. "Come with me."

Alan obeyed Jeanette and followed her. He walked alongside her in the garden. That paradise summer.

In the shadows, their moving figures vanished from the grounds. They came towards a marquee. They entered the marquee.

Their silhouettes were noticeable in the marquee. All alone, they spent time together in the marquee.

The flags blew in the wind.

They had a romantic time together on that enchanting summer evening.

Everybody else had been forbidden to enter the marquee at that time. Alan was King and Jeanette Queen that day. They both sat together on the throne. They were both quixotic and quizzical at that present time.

- THE END -

*Available worldwide from Amazon
and all good bookstores*

www.mtp.agency

www.facebook.com/mtp.agency

@mtp_agency

www.ingramcontent.com/pod-product-compliance
Lightning Source LLC
LaVergne TN
LVHW021736060526
838200LV00052B/3302